MR. GREEDY

by Roger Hargreaves

Copyright© 1971, 1980 by Roger Hargreaves
Published in U.S.A. by Price/Stern/Sloan Publishers, Inc.
410 North La Cienega Boulevard
Los Angeles, California 90048
Printed in U.S.A. All Rights Reserved.

ISBN: 0-8431-0817-7

PRICE/STERN/SLOAN
Publishers, Inc., Los Angeles

1983

Mr. Greedy liked to eat!

And the more he ate the fatter he became.

And the fatter he became the more hungry he became.

And the more hungry he became the more he ate.

And the more he ate the fatter he became.

And so it went on.

He lived in a house that looked much like he did.

A roly-poly sort of house!

One morning, Mr. Greedy awoke earlier than usual.

He'd been dreaming about food, as usual, and that caused him to wake up feeling hungry, as usual.

So, Mr. Greedy got up, went downstairs, and ate the most enormous breakfast.

This is what Mr. Greedy had for his breakfast.

TOAST — 2 slices

CORNFLAKES — 1 packet

MILK — 1 bottle

SUGAR — 1 bowlful

TOAST — 3 slices

EGGS — 3 boiled

TOAST — 4 slices

BUTTER — 1 dish

JELLY — 1 jar

Boy, was he greedy!

When he had finished his enormous breakfast, Mr. Greedy sat back in his chair and smiled a very satisfied smile.

"That was a delicious breakfast," he thought to himself. "Now I wonder what would be nice to have for lunch?"

He decided to work up an appetite for lunch by going for a long walk.

That morning, Mr. Greedy walked and walked.

Then he discovered a cave.

"That's funny," he thought, "I don't remember seeing that here before."

Being a curious sort of fellow, Mr. Greedy decided to explore.

He entered the dark cave.

Inside, he discovered some giant steps leading upwards.

Mr. Greedy, being a curious sort of fellow, decided to climb them.

They were very steep and difficult to climb, but, with much huffing and puffing, Mr. Greedy made his way to the top.

Once there, he came to a door.

It was, without a doubt, the biggest door that Mr. Greedy had ever seen. And it wasn't quite shut.

Mr. Greedy, being a curious sort of fellow, decided to see what was on the other side of that door.

He squeezed himself through the crack in the door, and there before him was an amazing sight.

The biggest room in the world!

The table in the middle of the room was as big as a house, and the chairs around it were as tall as trees.

Mr. Greedy felt very small.

Then he sniffed.

Coming from somewhere up on top of that gigantic table was the most delicious smell that Mr. Greedy had ever smelled.

Mr. Greedy sniffed again, and then decided that he must get up onto that table. So, he began to climb up the leg of the enormous chair.

It was very difficult, and it took him a long time. Eventually, though, Mr. Greedy stood on the table.

Everything was larger than life.

There was a bowl of fruit on the table, and Mr. Greedy tried to lift one of the oranges.

It was bigger than he was!

Mr. Greedy, being greedy, took a bite out of one of the apples there.

Then he looked around.

Over on the other side of the table stood the source of that delicious smell.

It was a huge, enormous, gigantic, colossal plate. And on the plate were huge, enormous, gigantic, colossal sausages the size of pillows, and huge, enormous, gigantic, colossal potatoes the size of beach balls, and huge, enormous, gigantic, colossal peas the size of cabbages.

Mr. Greedy hurried across the table toward the plate and, being Mr. Greedy, began to eat.

Suddenly, Mr. Greedy found himself being picked up by a giant's hand.

"AND WHO," thundered the giant, "ARE YOU?"

Mr. Greedy was so frightened that he could only manage to squeak his name.

The giant laughed a laugh as loud as thunder. "GREEDY BY NAME AND GREEDY BY NATURE," he bellowed. "YOU NEED TO BE TAUGHT A LESSON."

And what a lesson it was.

The giant made Mr. Greedy eat up everything on that huge, enormous, gigantic, colossal plate.

When he had finished, Mr. Greedy felt very ill indeed, as if he would burst at any minute.

"Now," said the giant in a much quieter voice, "do you promise never to be greedy again?"

"Oh yes," moaned Mr. Greedy, "I promise!"

"Very well," said the giant, "then I'll let you go."

Mr. Greedy climbed down from the table and went out through the door feeling very fat and extremely miserable.

And do you know, from that day to this, Mr. Greedy has kept his promise.

Mr. Greedy doesn't look like he used to look anymore.

He now looks like this, which I think suits him a lot better. Don't you?

So, if you know anybody who's as greedy as Mr. Greedy used to be, you know what to tell him don't you?

Beware of giants!